A

Disney
Adventures
THE MAGAZINE FOR KIDS

BOOK

UFO files

OUT OF THIS WORLD...
but true?

BY SEAN PLOTTNER

DISNEY PRESS

New York

Illustrations by Jim Phillips

Photo Credits
Cover
  Front (inset): copyright © Chip Simons
  Back (clockwise from right): copyright © Robin Thomas;
  courtesy of Archive Photos; courtesy of the Roswell Museum;
  copyright © Robin Thomas.
Interior
  Pp.1 (top and bottom), 17, 36, 39, 41, 88: courtesy of Archive
  Photos; pp. 1, 57: Jeff Scheid; pp. 3, 5, 18, 28, 55:
  copyright © Robin Thomas; pp. 44, 49, 78: copyright © Chip
  Simons; pp. 47, 81: courtesy of the Roswell Museum: p. 9
  copyright © PhotoDisc, Inc.

Printed in the United States of America.

First Edition
10 9 8 7 6 5 4 3 2 1

Library of Congress Catalog Card Number: 97-65681

ISBN: 0-7868-4146-X

Reprinted by arrangement with Disney Press.

CONTENTS

Introduction

 ysterious lights flash through the sky. A strange-looking craft hovers over a field.

Military radar picks up *something* that travels faster than any known aircraft.

Welcome to the great unknown—the world of mysterious, unidentified flying objects known as UFOs.

Since the beginning of time, people have gazed at unexplainable lights in the sky and wondered what they were. Imagine the first rainbow or shooting star. If you were the first to see it, how would you know what it was? With advances in science and technology, we've been able to identify many previously mysterious sightings. Still, we can't explain everything.

Like UFOs. Are they flying saucers, piloted by aliens from across the universe? Or are they just airplanes, weather balloons, or blimps that are mistaken for UFOs? If you want a good controversy, just ask your friends what they think. Few subjects get people talking—and arguing—like this one.

There's no doubt that UFOs exist. But are aliens behind the UFO mystery? No one has absolutely, definitively, *without question* proved that aliens exist or that they've visited Earth.

At least, not yet. By thinking critically and carefully examining evidence from all sides,

What is a UFO?

"A UFO is the reported sighting of an object or light seen in the sky or on land, whose appearance, trajectory, actions, motions, lights, and colors do not have a logical, conventional, or natural explanation, and which cannot be explained, not only by the original witness, but by scientists or technical experts who try to make a common sense identification after examining the evidence."
—*J. Allen Hynek, Center for UFO Studies (CUFOS)*

investigators like you could one day help settle this great mystery.

This book explores recent UFO sightings as well as some classic cases. It also tells you how real UFO investigators interview witnesses, examine evidence, and expose hoaxes. We'll also tell you what they believe—and don't believe—about many famous UFO cases.

UFOs—they're the most exciting mystery in the universe. Let's check 'em out.

Chapter One

Space Aliens—
FACT OR FICTION?

VESHAM, PENNSYLVANIA. 1994.
Mysterious red and orange lights streak across the night sky. A sudden electrical blackout knocks out light and power throughout the city. Panic strikes Kimberly Benninger, twelve. Huddled in her dark home, she fears that creatures from another planet are landing nearby.

Were the strange lights actually a UFO that caused this blackout, or was it just a freaky power outage?

IRAN. SEPTEMBER 19, 1976. Air Force officials report a large white light in the sky. They assume it's just a star, but they send a Phantom jet off to investigate anyway. As the Phantom approaches the light, the jet loses all radio and instrument power. When the

Waves of the Past

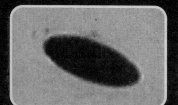

A time of extraordinary numbers of UFO sightings is known as a "wave" or "flap." According to UFO experts, UFO waves have occurred in the U.S. in 1947, 1952, 1957, 1966, 1973, and 1986—87.

pilot turns back for home, the plane's power suddenly returns.

A second Phantom jet takes off to pursue the light. The pilot tries to fire a missile from twenty-five miles away. But he can't—his plane has suffered a temporary power outage, too. Suddenly, a glowing object falls from the white light. It drops to the ground in a remote area and gives off a brilliant light that temporarily blinds the Phantom pilot. He turns for home.

The following day, officials find nothing at the landing site.

More aliens?

Maybe. Ufologists—investigators who study UFOs—could not find an explanation. The case remains unsolved.

Back in Evesham, investigators found a simple explanation the day after the blackout. Turns out a furry little creature from *this* planet—a raccoon—had crawled up on a transformer full of electrical switches. The poor critter sparked an electrical fire that lit up the sky with glowing flames and caused more than 19,000 homes to lose power for two hours.

The unlucky raccoon got fried.

What's Going On?

Witnesses all over the world report thousands of UFO encounters like these each year. But only a few UFOs remain unidentified. Most sightings, upon closer inspection, turn up a roasted raccoon or some other earthly explanation. IFOs, or identified flying objects like airplanes and birds, fool a lot of people. In fact, ufologists can trace about 95 percent of

> Most sightings, upon closer inspection, turn up a roasted raccoon or some other earthly explanation.

all UFO reports to human error. That means only five out of every one hundred cases go unsolved.

Surveys show that about half of all Americans believe

UFOs are "something real," and not just people's imaginations. But plenty of people disagree. Called skeptics, they claim that every UFO report has a simple explanation, even if we don't know what it is yet.

Both the UFO believers and UFO skeptics make convincing arguments. Here's a brief look at their key points.

UFO Skeptic: Excuse me, but there's no proof of intelligent life anywhere else in the universe.

UFO Believer: Oh, *puh-lease*. We can't be the only life in the universe. The conditions that led to life on Earth (a nearby sun and lots of water, for example) could occur on other planets.

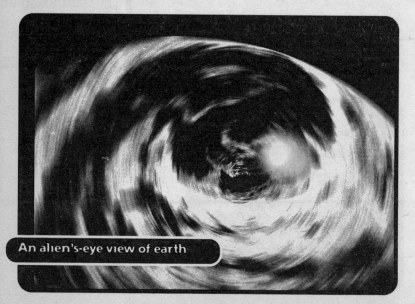

An alien's-eye view of earth

8

Many scientists agree. "The fact that we exist proves that the formation of life is possible," says physicist Lawrence Krauss. "Once we know that life can originate here, the likelihood of it occurring elsewhere is vastly increased."

Recent discoveries support this idea. In 1996, NASA researchers found potential evidence of life forms on Mars. Probes are headed to the Red Planet to search for more evidence. From October 1995 through October 1996 alone, astronomers discovered at least nine new planets, trillions of miles from Earth. Could they be home to an even more advanced form of life? Why not?

Prime Time

In the U.S., most UFO sightings occur around 9 P.M. or 3 A.M. and peak during the month of July. States in the Northeast and the Southwest report the greatest number of UFO sightings.

UFO Skeptic: Even if intelligent life existed on distant planets (and it doesn't!), it couldn't travel to Earth. No way. The laws of physics and the huge distances involved make interstellar travel impossible.

As far as we know, nothing travels faster than a beam

of light, which clocks in at 186,000 miles in one second, or six trillion miles in a year. It's hard to imagine that kind of speed, which would be required for humans to travel to distant planets. These examples may help:

- Moonlight takes around two seconds to reach the Earth, a distance of 240,000 miles.

- Sunlight takes eight minutes to travel the 93 million—mile journey to Earth.

If you could travel that fast, it would take you more than thirty-nine years to get to one of those new planets. If you could leave now, half your life would be over by the time you arrived!

UFO Believer: Why are you such a puny-brain? An alien civilization could be so much smarter than us and have such advanced technologies that it would have no problem traveling great distances. Right now, we don't think interstellar space travel is possible. But future inventors could one day change that.

UFO Skeptic: Even if intelligent life existed and could travel so far, the odds are against the aliens landing on Earth. There's just way, way too much space in the universe to explore. It's the old needle in the haystack, and the universe is one heckuva haystack!

UFO Believer: You're so human—you think we're the smartest creatures around! We might be pretty stupid compared to an alien race with bigger brains and such a superior intelligence that we can't even begin to understand it. Smart or dumb, aliens cruising around the universe could also get lucky and just bump into Earth!

Crop circles: messages from extraterrestrials?

UFO Skeptic: There's no good reason why an alien — if it existed — would want to visit Earth.

UFO Believer: C'mon, that's ridiculous. Aliens would visit Earth because, like us, they're curious. We send probes to explore other planets and if we could visit them in person we would.

Why wouldn't aliens do the same thing?

UFO Skeptic: Stars, planets, the moon, unusual atmospheric conditions, bizarre weather, satellites, unusual military aircraft, weather balloons, and even clouds are all regularly mistaken for UFOs. Face it, people are stupid. When you add human error to the equation, you can account for nine out of ten UFO reports. The remaining cases will eventually be explained, too.

UFO Believer: Sure, people make mistakes, but what

UFO . . .

about that tiny number of UFO cases that remains unsolved?

UFO Skeptic: There's no physical evidence of UFOs. Show me a knob from a UFO. Introduce me to an alien! Crop circles (intricate patterns in fields believed to be created by UFOs), landing marks, conversations with aliens, and all the other stories are either faked or misinterpreted.

UFO Believer: Sure, we don't have actual craft or aliens to show you, but crop circles and landing sites marked by burned grass are solid evidence of UFOs. The government may have solid evidence, too—but they won't share their secrets.

There aren't any simple solutions to the UFO mystery. But as any ufologist will tell you, it's important to keep an open mind. We don't know everything, and the

or IFO?

universe seems full of possibilities that we may find hard to accept.

Centuries ago, when Greek mathematicians first suggested the world was round, skeptics thought they were nutcases. When the astronomer Copernicus boldly declared the sun the center of our solar system, many considered him bonkers. And when Jules Verne wrote more than a hundred years ago that humans would travel to the moon, everyone laughed.

But wait—all of these men eventually proved to be right. So maybe the space alien theory should be considered as one of the many possible explanations to account for the UFO phenomenon.

The mystery—and the controversy—rages on.

Chapter Two

Close Encounters

What really happens when someone sees a UFO? To find out, check out the *Disney Adventures'* UFO Casefile.

Each of these UFO stories, selected from thousands of unsolved cases, can be grouped into one of the four major UFO sighting categories. The first is close encounter of the first kind. This is the most common type of UFO encounter reported,

> UFO stories can be grouped into one of the four major UFO categories.

and it's pretty basic: A witness sees a UFO (either a craft or mysterious lights) flying in the sky. It's that simple. Now let's examine some cases.

Camp UFO

Here's a typical Close Encounter of the First Kind. In April 1990, two Louisiana Boy Scout leaders took their troop on a camping trip. They arrived at their campground near a small lake around midnight. As the two leaders pitched a tent, they noticed a light moving just above the trees on the other side of the lake.

No big deal, they thought. Probably just an airplane. But when the light crossed the lake and stopped less than

The light crossed the lake and stopped less than 150 feet away from them.

150 feet away from them, they knew it was no airplane! One leader later reported that the UFO was about the same size as his fist when he stretched his arm out straight (a common way to measure UFO size). The light hovered for about a minute, completely silent. Then it took off and disappeared.

The leaders were frightened, to say the least. Forget the camping trip and working on merit badges: they immediately reported the sighting to the camp ranger. Eventually the scouts were interviewed by UFO investi-

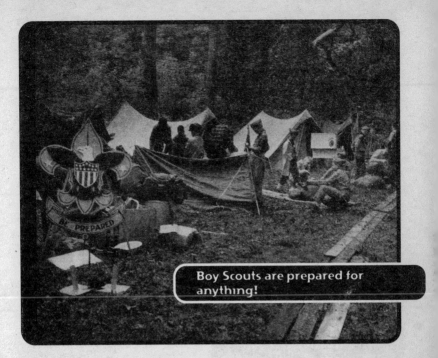

Boy Scouts are prepared for anything!

gators, who have yet to come up with an explanation.

The case remains unsolved.

Bullet in the Sky

Several people in Durant, Oklahoma, reported seeing a UFO on the night of August 25, 1992.

Martin Gladstone first saw the object at around 11 P.M. Looking out his bedroom window to the west, he saw what he thought was a plane. But instead of flying in a straight line, it was darting back and forth. The UFO also moved way too fast to be a plane.

Martin yelled to his wife and some friends who were visiting, and they rushed in to take a look.

THE BIRTH OF UFOS

The term UFO originated in 1956, when a former U.S. Air Force official wrote a book about flying saucer investigations he and other officials had conducted for the military. Called "The Report on Unidentified Flying Objects," it was the first time anyone used the words that were eventually shortened to "UFO."

"You ain't going to believe this," he told them, "but that is not a star. That is something else."

Everyone went outside for a better look. Martin's wife later described the object as being shaped "like the top of a bullet." It was pointed at the top and light rays came out of the flat bottom. She said it was all white.

Martin agreed with his wife about the UFO's shape, but reported seeing three colors. He said the object was blue on top, yellow in the middle, and white on the bottom.

A trained UFO investigator interviewed the four witnesses separately. They all reported seeing the same thing, although one of Martin's friends admitted that she was not wearing her glasses at the time of the sighting.

Like most people who study UFOs, the investigator was skeptical. After all, it would be nice if

> It was pointed at the top and light rays came out of the flat bottom.

witnesses would put on their glasses before making a report. However, he didn't feel the witnesses were lying. They seemed intelligent and honest, and none of them had read much about UFOs, which could have led them to judge what they saw too quickly.

The case remains unsolved.

CASE Nº 3:

The Chase Is On!

On April 18, 1966, near Ravenna, Ohio, hundreds of people reported seeing a "brilliant and shiny" UFO flying overhead. Deputy sheriff Dale Spaur and partner W. H. Neff had the closest encounter with the object, and it led to the chase of their lives.

That night, the two lawmen were checking out a car

that had been abandoned along a rural highway. They saw radio equipment inside the car and a strange logo—a triangle around a bolt of lightning—on one door.

Suddenly they heard a bizarre humming noise behind them. They turned around to see a huge saucer-shaped craft rising out of some nearby woods. It hovered above them and covered them in warm white light before flying off.

When the deputies came to their senses, they ran to

their cruiser and gave chase. Now it's a little crazy to chase a UFO—what do you do if you catch up? Dale hit speeds close to one hundred miles an hour as he drove after it. Only after eighty-six miles of pursuit did Dale run out of gas. Then, as Dale and his partner watched, the UFO started going straight up. Dale said it had a large dome on top, where an antenna was sticking out, and guessed that it measured about fifty feet across and twenty feet high. The UFO took off.

"We were close, closer than I ever want to be again," Dale later told a newspaper reporter. "I know nobody's going to believe it, but it's true. It wasn't just an object floating around. It could maneuver. The only sound was a steady, faint humming, like an electrical transformer, when we first spotted it." The craft made no noise during the chase.

> "The only sound was a steady, faint humming, like an electrical transformer, when we first spotted it." The craft made no noise during the chase.

The next day, investigators checked with the Federal Aviation Administration's two air traffic control centers in the area. Neither had spotted any unknown objects on radar.

Was the craft somehow connected with the mystery car the deputies had stopped to inspect? No one knows—the car was never seen again. But the UFO was.

Two months later, Dale was driving down a different road one night. He looked up and couldn't believe his eyes—there was the UFO!

He parked his car and sat there, staring at the floor, too afraid to look up. People had made fun of him for reporting his first UFO sighting, and he didn't want that again. After fifteen minutes, Dale finally peeked. The UFO had disappeared, never to be seen again.

The Birth of Flying Saucers

One of the most famous Close Encounters of the First Kind took place back in 1947. Kenneth Arnold, a businessman, was flying his small plane one afternoon from Chehalis, Washington, to nearby Yakima. It was an average flight until several flashes of light caught the pilot's eye. Off to the north, Kenneth saw a formation of bright objects coming from Mt. Baker. There were nine of them, flying right over the mountains and "traveling at tremendous speed," he later reported. "I watched as these objects rapidly neared Mt. Rainier, all the time thinking to myself that I was observing a whole formation of jets. They were flying in formation. What startled me most at this point was the fact that I could not find any tails on them."

> There were nine of them, flying right over the mountains and "traveling at tremendous speed."

As Kenneth watched the objects, he tried to judge how quickly they were moving by timing them with his cockpit clock. He determined they were cruising at an amazing 1,700 miles an hour! He also opened his canopy to make sure what he was witnessing was not caused by sunlight reflecting off the canopy. It wasn't.

After he landed, Kenneth sketched what he had seen and reported his sighting to investigators. "They flew like a saucer would if you skipped it across water," he said. (In other words, they looked like a stone you skip across a lake.) He didn't say he saw flying saucers, but that's exactly what the press reported. The rest is history, and flying saucers became the common way to describe UFOs.

> He determined they were cruising at an amazing 1,700 miles an hour!

No one ever identified the mysterious objects. Dr. Allen Hynek, one of the earliest UFO investigators, speculated that Kenneth actually saw a flock of birds that were reflecting strong sunlight. This was never proven, although numerous reports of UFOs flying in formation since that time have turned out to be exactly that.

Kenneth, a respected businessman and a skilled pilot, seemed believable. The media covered his story extensively, creating worldwide interest in UFOs. As the news spread, more people stepped forward with their own UFO reports, which is why many UFO experts consider this case the beginning of the modern UFO era.

——————————————○—○—○

Alien Boomerang

Okay, so not all UFOs are flying saucers. How about flying boomerangs? More than one person reported seeing a huge, boomerang-shaped craft with lights over the skies of southern Florida in early 1993.

> A U-shaped object with bluish-white lights moved through the sky.

"A Stealth fighter, maybe? Swamp gas? Aerobatic planes flying in formation?" asked a local newspaper in an article about the sightings. Or a UFO? Once the paper published the story, more than ten other people called to say they'd seen something similar.

"It was moving pretty steady, kind of streaking through the sky," said Linda Lawrence of Clearwater. At

The Truth is Out There

8:30 P.M. on April 27, she saw a V-shaped object with bluish-white lights moving through the sky. "It was gone in a minute or two. I didn't know what it was. It didn't look like a plane or a helicopter. I didn't immediately think UFO. Tell people you saw a UFO and they think you're crazy."

Two local UFO investigators, Eugene and Jean Brown, decided to investigate. They found witnesses in two counties and listened to their stories. "I think these people are definitely seeing something real," Jean reported.

Could the boomerang have been a top-secret U.S. military plane? Some people think so. A 1991 magazine article had claimed the government was testing a "black, silent boomerang-shaped vehicle that stretches between 600 and 800 feet across." This aircraft supposedly uses "constellation camouflage"— lights on the hull that look just like stars. The plane can hover

This aircraft supposedly uses "constellation camouflage."

and rotate in place, according to the article.

The military says such a plane does not exist. Of course, if it's a big secret, why would they say anything else?

Classify this as yet another unexplained Close Encounter of the First Kind.

CASE N⁰. 6:

The Mystery Blob

You never know when a UFO might appear. It could even happen while you're walking to school.

That's exactly what thirteen-year-old Joe De Guevara, of Anaheim, California, was doing in the early morning of February 9, 1995. At about 6:45 A.M., Joe noticed something strange in the sky.

"It was all different shapes, not just one," he later told a newspaper reporter. "It wasn't really round, it wasn't really square. It looked like two people on top of a platform, spinning."

Joe continued on his way to Ball Junior High, watching the UFO the whole way. When he arrived, he noticed a small crowd of students and teachers gathered outside, staring at the UFO. "It was like a cylinder, black, turning and rotating in the sky," said Alexandra Diaz, fourteen.

"We feel strange admitting we saw something so weird in the sky," said Elaine Mazor, the school's attendance clerk. She described the UFO as two dark, long objects hovering over the school. "I didn't see any green men or anything," she added.

> A small crowd of students and teachers gathered outside, staring at the UFO.

As you can tell, Elaine's description differed from the kids' accounts, making it more difficult for investigators to figure out what happened. (Eyewitness reports often vary like this, making them seem unreliable.)

A former World War II pilot, seventy-two-year-old Chris Christensen, also saw the Anaheim mystery craft. Chris, who lived about a mile from the school, saw the UFO at 7:30 A.M., when he went outside to pick up the newspaper. "I grabbed my binoculars," he said. "I was

just curious. It was like a piece of junk hanging from an invisible balloon. To me it looked like an old car that got hit by a freight train, but I still don't have the slightest idea what it was. You don't usually see something floating in the sky like that."

UFO investigator Melinda Leslie first checked with Disneyland, just three miles away. Was some celebration there responsible for the UFO?

"It wasn't Disneyland," said a Magic Kingdom executive. "I checked with everyone who might have conceivably had something in the air this morning, and no one did."

Forget the Disney explanation.

Okay, how about the airport five miles away? Investigators found that the Federal Aviation Administration (FAA) had received no reports about UFO sightings. Airport controllers said they'd seen nothing unusual in the air that morning.

Forget the weird airplane explanation.

Meteorologist Stephen Ahn told the investigator that the National Weather Service, where he worked, regularly released weather balloons to test atmospheric conditions. But never in Orange County, where the UFO sightings took place.

> Forget the military explanation. So what was it?

Forget the weather balloon explanation.

Next, investigators checked with El Toro Marine Corps Air Station and Tustin Marine Air Corps Station. No planes flew out of El Toro before 8 A.M. that morning, and the first helicopters to take off from Tustin left around 8 A.M.

Forget the military explanation.

So what was it? "We don't know, in fact, that it was extraterrestrial," Melinda, the investigator, said. But she doesn't have any definite answers. And without any, this case remains a UFO.

Chapter Three

Bizarre Evidence

Close encounter of the second kind: a UFO not only appears but also leaves behind some sort of physical evidence, such as landing marks, broken tree branches, or crop circles.

CASE NO. 7:

Crash at Sunrise Highway

Crash landing! Some ufologists claim that UFOs have actually crashed on Earth—but no one has ever produced any wreckage. Still, the stories are bizarre enough to make you at least wonder what could have happened.

One crash supposedly took place on Long Island, New York, on the night of November 24, 1991. Several drivers on Sunrise Highway thought they saw a plane going down into a remote part of Southaven Park in Shirley. People living near the park also reported hearing loud rumbles and seeing strange lights.

Someone reported a fire, and roads around the park were quickly blocked off by police. But local firemen were turned back. Instead, firefighters from a nearby

U.S. government laboratory handled the emergency.

For the next four days, the park remained sealed off. During that time, a neighbor reported strange happenings at his house. He told local UFO investigator John Ford that his phone rang "strangely," and when he answered, no one was on the other end. He also said park rangers had told him the park was shut down to the public because it was reserved for duck hunting that week.

After the park reopened, John and a team of ufologists went in for a look around. "We found an area that was burned out, and some trees were bent over," he reported. "A section looked like it had been plowed over by machinery. We were getting a higher than normal radiation reading in the area." He also found that a nearby metal fence had no magnetic reading. All metal fences, he explained, should contain a magnetic charge from the Earth. "Something had stripped away the fence's magnetic charge," John said.

> John and a team of ufologists went in for a look around.

A year later, John showed a videotape of what he believes was the UFO crash site. It's fuzzy, and John wouldn't say where he got it. The local newspaper obtained a copy and, after viewing it, published this report:

"The video shows people examining a bright reddish, metallic-type object about four square feet that appears to be emitting a white, cloudy gas, and a hissing sound can be heard—a sight and sound that resembles dry ice that has been exposed to warmer temperatures. The next shot shows what appears to be a person trying to lift up a body near a tree, but the poor quality of the film makes positive identification impossible. In a final scene, three uniformed men (wearing dark jackets and rounded caps similar to federal S.W.A.T. teams) are seen placing a large, shiny spread over something on the ground."

> "We are still very actively investigating this event."

The video wasn't good enough to prove anything. Photographs and videos are too easy to fake and misread, so they rarely make strong UFO evidence.

To this day, no one has come forward with further evidence or information about what happened in Southaven Park.

"We are still very actively investigating this event," explains John. "We believe that an extraterrestrial craft, with aliens, crashed that night in the park—and we are out to prove it."

But so far, they haven't.

Car Stops

Most people feel pretty safe in their cars. After all, they can always make a quick getaway in case of an emergency. But not if there's a UFO in the neighborhood!

Investigators have speculated that UFOs produce strange magnetic and electric fields that cripple the operation of engines or other power sources. These are called "car stops," although airplanes and other machines may also be affected.

Collecting Crop Circle Evidence

If you happen to come across a crop circle, you can send a plant sample to ufologist Linda Moulton-Howe for analysis. Here's how:

1. At the center of the circle, dig up some of the pressed vegetation. Use a garden trowel and be sure to dig down one inch so you can include roots and soil.

2. Place the roots and soil in a plastic bag. Secure it, even if plant stalks have to stick out (tape the top together if necessary).

3. With a dark marker, label the bag with this info: the date the circle was found, the date you collected plants, exact location of the middle of the circle, your name, address, and phone number.

4. From the middle of the circle, walk one city block's distance in any direction and collect and label another sample. Return to the middle and walk another block's distance in the opposite direction to collect and label another sample.

5. Send samples in a long-stemmed—rose box (available at florists) to: Linda Moulton-Howe, P.O. Box 538, Huntingdon Valley, PA 19006. Include a map of the area with the crop circle location marked on it if possible. Linda and other scientists will examine your evidence and use it to further their understanding of crop circles.

Skeptics say that cars and planes break down every day. Why blame UFOs? Well, because of cases like these:

🛸 **November 2, 1957:** At least twenty people near Levelland, Texas, report separate Close Encounters of the Second Kind. Witnesses include policemen, firefighters, and several people who were driving cars at the time. All describe the same thing: a brilliant, glowing object in the sky. At the same time, just about every car and truck involved lost power. One driver says his headlights even flashed on and off in rhythm with the pulsing of an egg-shaped UFO. "When the UFO got nearer," another witness reported, "the lights of my truck went out and the motor died. I jumped out and hit the deck as the thing

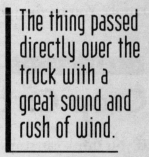

The thing passed directly over the truck with a great sound and rush of wind.

passed directly over the truck with a great sound and rush of wind. It sounded like thunder, and my truck rocked. I felt a lot of heat." After the UFO took off, all power returned to the vehicles.

🛸 **April 1974:** Three people driving in Belgium see a brightly lit round object in the sky. Suddenly their car engine dies. They cannot start it until a couple of minutes later, after the UFO flies away.

August 1995: Around midnight, an Argentinian Airlines flight crew reports a UFO with shining lights approaching their plane. Many of the 103 passengers also see the object as they get near the airport. As the jet approaches the runway, intruments in the control tower go wacko. The airport loses all power, and the jet pilot needs two attempts before successfully landing on the darkened runway.

Do these accounts sound like your basic car problems? Or are they Close Encounters of the Second Kind? You be the judge.

CASE Nº. 9:

Crop Circles

If you think car stops are weird, hang on. Some people believe aliens use fields as giant doodle pads where they leave pictures and messages. If that's true, well, the aliens aren't doing a very good job of communicating, because no one can figure out what the messages mean.

Still, when huge circular areas of cut and flattened vegetation mysteriously appear in fields overnight, often with elaborate geometric patterns that look beautiful when viewed from the air, you gotta think something weird is going on.

Are these "saucer nests" or "crop circles" formed when a UFO lands? No-body knows! But there's no denying that thousands show up in fields around the world all the time. And about one out of every five appears after the sighting of strange lights or a UFO.

"It's highly probable a UFO connection exists," says one ufologist who studies crop circles. "But how are they made? By invisible UFOs? By an energy source coming from a craft so high up it can't be seen?"

Crop Circle Capitol

Wiltshire, a farming area in southwest England, tops the crop circle list. Each year, hundreds of beautiful circles appear here, far more than anywhere else in the world. Investigators still don't know why.

Crop circles first showed up in England in 1678. It wasn't until more recently, however, that crop circles started appearing worldwide. The mystery really heated up in 1980, when they started appearing throughout southern England, an area of the world now considered the hot spot for crop circles. Hundreds of circles appear there each year.

The smallest circle investigated was just eight inches around. The largest was nearly an eighth of a mile long. The intricate patterns include bars, triangles, and rings. Usually, the vegetation is swirled flat. Stalks are usually, but not always, bent low to the ground, but not broken off. Most of the time, the vegetation within a circle remains healthy and, even though the stalks are bent, continues to grow and thrive within the circle.

Scientists who have analyzed crop circles often find deformed seeds that are bent and twisted out of their normal shape. They've also measured radiation inside the circles. One scientist placed some normal wheat stalks in a microwave oven for a few minutes. When he removed the stalks, they had many of the same characteristics as those found in a crop circle. This means some sort of microwave-type energy could be behind crop circles. But who—or what—is behind this unusual energy force?

> "It's highly probable a UFO connection exists."

In photos taken from the air, some crop circles look like elaborate drawings done by a spirograph. They come in so many different patterns that some crop circle researchers give them names, like "The Bee," "The Claw," and "The Bicycle."

Is this the work of a UFO . . . or a lawnmower?

"To stand in one is unlike anything you've ever experienced," says crop circle investigator Linda Moulton-Howe. "The perfection takes your breath away."

Some ufologists think crop circles may be some sort of space alien communication with humans. Mathematicians who have studied the more complex circles say they show strange mathematical traits that could indicate some sort of numerical language. But no one knows what the geometric patterns mean.

"Could they be a way for E.T. to gradually introduce

himself?" wonders Linda Moulton-Howe. "Some people even believe that if you create your own crop circle, it's like writing a message back to aliens."

| Hundreds of circles appear each year. | Other theories also have been suggested, some that are silly. And of course, some crop circles are fakes. But then there's the Plasma Vortex |

Theory. This unproven notion speculates that electrified wind, called plasma, forms mini-tornadoes that screw down into fields to create patterns. As if anyone would believe that's what's behind the intricate patterns.

Crop circles are mysterious, beautiful, and fascinating. But if they're messages of some kind, we still don't have a clue what they say. Sure would be nice to know!

42

Chapter Four

Meet the Aliens

Close encounter of the third kind: a sighting of both a UFO and alien creatures. This is the rarest type of close encounter.

CASE Nº. 10:

They've Landed

This story involves a giant egg and a highway patrol officer in New Mexico, as only a UFO story could.

The officer, a respected citizen of his community, was considered an extremely believable witness, Still, his story sounds incredible.

On April 24, 1964, Officer Lonnie Zamora gave

Take me to your leader . . .

chase to a speeding car near Socorro, New Mexico, at
5:45 P.M. As he drove, Zamora heard an explosion and
saw what he later described as a bluish "flame in the
sky" about a mile away. He gave up on the speeder and
drove toward the explosion until he came to an area
full of boulders.

There he found a metallic egg-shaped craft. It was
about the size of a car and was sitting in a gulley. Two
humanlike figures stood next to it. They wore white

coveralls. One seemed surprised to see Zamora. Thinking maybe this was a car accident, Zamora drove to within one hundred feet of the craft. He radioed a possible accident to the sheriff's office and got out of his car.

Then he heard three loud slams similar to a door being shut. By the time he looked over at the "accident," blue flames were shooting out of the bottom of the craft. The officer, fearing for his life, hid behind his car. When he looked toward the craft again it was already in the air, not very high but flying away. He also noticed a strange red symbol on the door.

Another highway patrolman had heard Zamora's radio reports and attempted to find his fellow officer. Unfortunately, Sergeant Chavez made a wrong turn while driving to the site. If he hadn't done this, Chavez would probably have arrived while the UFO was still on the ground. Instead, he showed up only to find Zamora freaking out and staring at a smoking bush and four holes pressed into the soil from the craft's landing legs.

> **Blue flames were shooting out of the bottom of the craft.**

The U.S. Air Force opened an investigation but found nothing to dispute the patrol officers' story. In addition, at least five other witnesses came forward to say they too had seen either weird lights or a strange low-flying craft in the area. While skeptics later claimed this was a hoax, respected ufologists like Dr. Allen Hynek believed it was true. Impressed with the evidence and believable witnesses, Hynek called this case "one of the major UFO sightings in the history of the Air Force's consideration of this subject."

Roswell

You've probably heard of this most famous of UFO cases—it's the granddaddy of them all. While the debate still rages over what *really* happened near Roswell, New Mexico, in early July 1947, here's a look at what we do know.

On July 2, rancher William Brazel heard a huge explosion during an intense rainstorm. The next day, he found some strange bits of wreckage on his land. The shiny pieces he recovered looked like metal but were lightweight, like balsa wood. Brazel could easily bend the pieces, but when he tried to smash one with a sledgehammer, he couldn't even put

> On July 2, rancher William Brazel heard a huge explosion.

RECORD PHONES
Business Office 2288
News Department 2287

Daily Record

NEW MEXICO. TUESDAY, JULY 8, 1947

5c PER COPY.

AAF Captures Flying Saucer on Ranch in Roswell Region

Ex-King Carol Weds Mme. Lupescu

ouse Passes
x Slash by
arge Margin

Defeat Amendment
By Demos to Remove
Many from Rolls

Washington, July 8 (AP)—The
house passed today the Republican
sponsored bill to cut income
$4,000,000,000 annually beginnin

Security Council
Paves Way to Talks
On Arms Reductions

Lake Success, July 8 (AP)—The
United Nations security council
today approved an American blue-
print for arms reduction discus-
sions for a fourteen nations
warning that the plan would bring about
that the collapse of arms reduction
efforts.

The vote was 9 to 6, with Russia and Poland abstaining

In view of Russia's firm stand
realized she might paralyze the big
power veto to block the plan

Soviet Deputy Foreign Minister
issued A Gromyko gave his warning. A United Nations few effort to

No Details of Flying Disk Are Revealed

Roswell Hardware
Man and Wife
Report Disk Seen

The intelligence office of the
509th Bombardment group at Roswell Army Air Field announced at
noon today that the field has
come into possession of a flying
saucer.

According to information released by the
authority of Maj. J. A. Marcel,
intelligence officer, the disk was
recovered on a ranch in the Roswell
vicinity, after an unidentified
rancher had notified Sheriff Geo.
Wilcox, here, that he had found the
detail from ranch

Carol of Romania,
rica boun

Inquiring minds want to know . . . the truth.

a dent in it. Weirder yet, he noticed strange symbols on some of the bits.

The rancher called nearby Roswell Air Force Base to report what he'd found. Intelligence officer Jesse Marcel drove out, picked up the debris, and took it back to the base. His commander told him to put together a press release notifying reporters and the public that a real flying saucer had been found! The wreckage supposedly belonged to a flying saucer that had crashed several miles away. According to some stories, the Air Force had found the crashed saucer, along with several hurt or dead space aliens. The saucer was to be flown to Wright Patterson Air Force Base in Dayton, Ohio, for further investigation.

Then, in an amazing reversal, the Air Force denied everything the next day. The first press release was replaced by another one claiming that the wreckage actually came from a secret weather balloon being tested by the military. Sorry for the mistake, the release said!

But UFO investigators refused to give up. They conducted extensive interviews, hoping to find out what really happened. In *Crash at Corona*, a book written in 1992, investigators Stanton Friedman and William Moore argued that the weather balloon was indeed a cover-up story intended to mislead people. But what was being covered up?

> In an amazing reversal, the Air Force denied everything.

Roswell funeral home director Glenn Dennis had received an odd call from the air base on July 7. A man wanted to know if Dennis had any baby caskets, three to four feet long. "I told him we had two," Dennis told investigators. "He asked how long it would take to get more. I told him by the next morning."

An hour later, the same man called back and asked a

Roswell Museums

The International UFO Museum and Research Center

The better of the two, this hot spot features interesting exhibits, a library, and a display of the alleged Roswell crash victims.
Address: 400-402 North Main,
P.O. Box 2221, Roswell, NM 88202

UFO Enigma Museum

The main attraction here is a large re-creation of the crash site. Also available: info on tours to the real crash site.
Address: 6108 South Main,
P.O. Box 6047, Roswell, NM 88202

few questions about how to preserve dead bodies that had been lying outside for a while.

Another hour passed. Dennis received an emergency call to aid an injured motorcycle driver who happened to live on the base. Dennis drove the hurt rider to the base and dropped him off at the hospital, where he noticed a vehicle with lots of debris piled around it. According to Dennis, some of the wreckage had strange markings on it, like Egyptian hieroglyphics.

"Looks like you had a crash," he said to a captain.

"Get this man out of here," the captain ordered two military policemen.

Dennis was escorted off the base immediately, but not before a nurse friend of his came running out of a nearby examination room. White as a ghost, she yelled to the funeral director, "Glenn! Get out of here as fast as you can!"

Dennis later called the nurse friend and eventually met with her to see if she was okay. That's when she told him a bizarre tale.

That day at the base, she had been ordered to assist two doctors in a most unusual examination—of two alien creatures supposedly recovered from a flying saucer crash! "She said the doctors told her there was nothing in the medical textbooks to cover what they had," Dennis told a reporter in 1995. "She also overheard them say the bodies were found with or in some wreckage two or three miles from where everything else was located."

> The nurse described the mangled bodies of the strange creatures to Dennis.

The nurse described the mangled bodies of the strange creatures to Dennis. They had only four fingers on each hand. They were short and had little slits for mouths. The heads were unusually large and the arms somewhat small. "She said it was horrible," continued Dennis. "Then they all got sick and had to leave the room. That's when we met."

Dennis never saw the nurse again, and he believes she was transferred away.

Did the government find a crashed saucer and dead aliens? Were they examined at the air base? The military denies any such thing.

A new twist to the story arrived nearly fifty years later, when a film, supposedly showing an examination of one of the dead aliens, surfaced. The person who found the film gave little information about where he got it. The astounding film aired on television in 1995, entitled *Alien Autopsy: Fact or Fiction?* As you'll learn in chapter seven, the autopsy footage is generally considered a hoax.

Something strange happened in Roswell. The wreckage found by Brazel, the hastily concocted weather balloon story, and Glenn Dennis's testimony make this the most phenomenal—and still unsolved—case in UFO history.

CASE Nº. 12:

The Gulf Breeze Photos

This famous case produced some of the most incredible UFO pictures ever taken and turned the Florida panhandle into one of the hottest UFO spots in the world.

It's also brought a good deal of attention—and money—to a man named Ed Walters. The money angle makes some people wonder if he faked the whole story.

It all started when Walters gave five stunning Polaroids of UFOs to the *Gulf Breeze Sentinel* in November 1987. When they were published, others in the area came forward to say they had also seen the UFO. Soon, TV stations and newspapers, including the free-spending *National Enquirer*, beat a path to Gulf Breeze to get the story. More pictures turned up, showing the same UFO. Some had been taken with a toy camera that happened to be in Walter's car at the time of his close encounter.

Walters claimed that he'd had several similar encounters. One time, a blue beam shot out of a UFO and paralyzed him. At other times, space aliens communicated by putting voices in his head. Interestingly enough, they spoke Spanish.

> Walters also claimed the UFOs were "as big as a house."

He produced a shaky videotape of a UFO jerking from left to right, which he said he shot from behind some bushes in his backyard.

Investigators swooped in and they found disturbing evidence that the photos were faked. For one thing, the film used in a Polaroid camera is extremely slow, which means any object in motion would appear blurry when photographed. Although Walters said the UFOs were in constant motion, they're crystal clear in the Polaroids. Walters also claimed the UFOs were "as big as a house," but this could not be proven from looking at the video or photos. Investigators also asked why he hadn't used a better camera and film, especially since he claimed to "sense" sometimes that the UFOs were coming.

Some UFO analysts who checked the photos said they look suspicious. Other experts insisted the photos were real and that the object they showed could not be faked.

But What If E.T. Doesn't Drive?

In April 1996, Nevada renamed a 98-mile stretch of State Route 350 because of nearby Nellis Air Force Base and the infamous Area 51, where some conspiracy theorists believe the government houses an alien craft and crew. The road now goes by the official name of "Extraterrestrial Highway."

If the Gulf Breeze sightings, as they've come to be called, are a hoax, then why did Walters do it? That's simple, say the skeptics: he benefited from the intense publicity and brisk sales of the books he wrote about his UFO experiences.

But are you ready for this? UFO sightings continue to

this day in Gulf Breeze. Skywatchers hang out along a waterfront park each night, and occasionally strange lights do appear, creating much excitement. They've been filmed and photographed dozens of times. But they have never been fully explained.

Area 51 and Groom Lake

Some of the wildest UFO stories focus on remote U.S. military bases. One such base is Area 51, an ultrasecret

> Some of the crazier UFO proponets believe the government has a treaty with space aliens.

Air Force testing site in Nevada near Groom Lake. Numerous secret planes have been developed there. Everyone knows it exists, even though the government won't admit it.

Endless rumors circulate about crashed flying saucers and space aliens who secretly live and work there. Some of the crazier UFO proponents believe the government has a treaty with space aliens and lets them fly around in their UFOs without interfer-

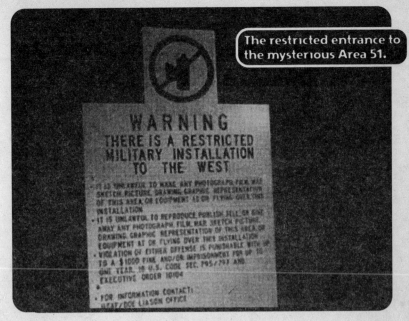

WARNING
THERE IS A RESTRICTED
MILITARY INSTALLATION
TO THE WEST

ence. In return, the aliens teach their advanced technology at the secret base.

Another story claims that you can find several alien saucers hidden in hangars at Nellis Range, another secret base in Nevada. Engineers there are supposedly trying to figure out how they work. A man named Bob Lazar claimed in 1989 he'd been working on the hush-hush project.

Conspiracies like these make fascinating, exciting stories. But they're pretty flimsy when you look closely. These bases are shrouded in secrecy for good reason: some of our country's biggest military projects are developed there. Any mysterious lights or craft in the skies near these bases probably come from ultrasecret new planes being test-flown by hotshot pilots, not from flying saucers. These planes probably look and fly dramatically differently from normal planes. That would make them UFOs, sure—but UFOs of human origin!

But people still flock to Area 51—known as The Ranch—with hopes of sighting a UFO. They gather at a spooky black mailbox in Rachel, Nevada, to scan the skies and swap stories. A whole tourist industry has cropped up to feed and house them. Since they *want* to see something but can't get close to the base, rumors run rampant. But no one has ever produced evidence of a UFO or alien cover-up at any of these bases.

Chapter Five

Abduction

 Close encounter of the fourth kind: people are contacted by space aliens and, against their will, are mysteriously transported into extraterrestrial spacecraft. It may be several hours before the human is released, with no memory of the experience. Only through hypnosis is the encounter remembered.

WARNING: Close Encounters of the Fourth Kind are the scariest alien encounters that have been reported. For the past thirty years, investigators have heard thousands of reports about a variety of frightening and highly personal alien encounters. Every report is different, but ufologists say an abduction encounter usually follows this pattern:

Someone driving alone at night sees a strange light or shadow. She stops to look. Next thing she knows, aliens, or a beam of light, take her away to a silent, cold room where she's examined. Sometimes the aliens "speak" directly to her mind telepathically. They've been known to tell her the dangers of nuclear war or destroying the Earth's environment.

Then, as the witness "wakes up" back in her car, she sees the UFO flying off. Eventually she realizes *something* weird happened, even though she can't remember any details. This is called Missing Time Experience (MTE). Back home, she may have bad dreams or find a new scar or mark on her body. Later on, she may remember everything that happened. More frequently, however, doctors trained in hypnosis put people who have had MTEs in a deep trance, and the witnesses are able to recall their alien experiences.

These abduction stories can be scary and puzzling. Are aliens "borrowing" humans for their experiments? Are they trying to warn us about the end of the world? Can they control our thoughts and memories? No one knows. And no victim has ever brought back a souvenir, so there's no proof that the abduction happened. Skeptics insist that people hear about alien abductions on TV and convince themselves they experienced one.

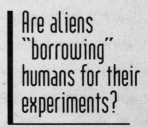

Are aliens "borrowing" humans for their experiments?

Once again, we have all the elements of a great mystery: no proof, plenty of controversy, and amazing stories like the ones you're about to read.

CASE NO. 14:

Betty and Barney Hill

The first well-known Close Encounter of the Fourth Kind involved a grandmotherly woman named Betty Hill. She and her husband, Barney, were on their way home from a vacation on September 19, 1961. It was late at night in the New Hampshire mountains when they spotted what they thought was a big, bright star—only this star was blinking and darting around. Then it stopped in midair over their car. The Hills saw a flying craft with double rows of windows and humanoid figures inside. The Hills sped away and turned off the main highway to get away.

Next thing they knew, they were safe and sound at home.

But two years later, after a series of nightmares and ulcers, the Hills remembered bits and pieces of that night. They let a psychiatrist hypnotize them. That's when they recalled turning off the highway and finding space aliens standing in the road. The aliens stopped them, took them aboard their ship, and examined them. Betty even had a conversation with the spaceship's captain.

> They had very large eyes that went around to the side of their head and slanted upward.

Betty was the first person to describe aliens as little grey men—the "Greys" as they are called now because so many people describe the same kind of space alien. "They were short, about four and a half feet tall, with grey skin color," Betty said. "They were dressed in dark one-piece outfits, no buttons, no insignias. They wore small caps, almost military. I did not see hair or ears. They had very large eyes that went around to the side of their head and slanted upward. They had a very small nose, and just a thin slit for a mouth."

The space alien "captain" told the Hills that they

would not be harmed. "The examiner was tugging on my teeth," Betty continued. "The leader asked me why Barney's teeth were removable and why mine were not (Barney wore dentures). That's when I started talking with the leader. I tried to tell him why teeth were removable. I told him about diet and age. The leader was curious about what age and time were. But I couldn't make him understand what I was saying."

Eventually, the Hills were led back to their car, and

the ship took off. Back in their car, the Hills found their dog, Dulcey, cowering under the front seat.

Their story got lots of publicity, and Betty Hill became a celebrity, appearing in magazines and giving speeches. Even though their abduction was the first one widely publicized, many people believed the Hills, partly because they did not immediately remember the encounter. Today, however, skeptics think that hypnosis is not reliable. And the fact that the Hills made money from a movie and other publicity about their encounter casts doubt on their story.

> The Hills found their dog, Dulcey, cowering under the front seat.

One thing is certain: thousands of abduction cases are reported each year. And it all started with Betty and Barney Hill.

CASE NO. 15:

The Hudson Wave

Poor Joe Dolan. All he wanted to do was drive home. But those darn aliens weren't going to let it happen.

The place is New York's Hudson Valley, where witnesses report hundreds of UFO sightings each year.

Many are abduction cases, or Close Encounters of the Fourth Kind. UFO investigator Philip J. Imbrogno has studied about a hundred of these incidents, including the mysterious abduction of Joe Dolan.

Dolan, a computer scientist in his early twenties, was driving home to New Castle, New York, at 10 P.M. on the night of March 13, 1988. His route took him along Highway 116 in Croton Falls, a dark, creepy road through the woods. As he came to a large reservoir, Dolan noticed bright white lights out over the water. They looked too low to be an airplane, but Dolan  wasn't sure. So he slowed down, peering through the trees at the lights while he drove. When he came to a clearing, he stopped.

Dolan rolled down the window as the lights came closer to his car. He leaned halfway out the window. The lights seemed to be emanating from a dark object, which made no sound even though it was now just twenty feet above the treetops. The UFO slowly flew over his car, giving Dolan a clearer view. It was a triangle-shaped object, about one hundred feet long. The lights were only on the front, although he noticed flashes—like

Alien Races

Here are some of the aliens reportedly out there:

GREYS: The most common alien type reported. Greys stand about three feet tall with black slanted eyes, no pupils, a tiny nose and mouth, and large heads. Their greyish-whitish bodies are hairless. Many people believe the Greys abduct humans and teach highly advanced technology secrets to our government!

REPTOIDS: A nasty reptile-like race of aliens that competes with Greys. Some people think they're even controlling the Greys—but not because they like humans!

BLUES: The good guys, these aliens are described as having see-through skin, large almond-shaped eyes, and tiny bodies. They're supposedly visiting Earth to warn us about the Greys.

HUMANOIDS: Encounters with these child like, part-alien, part-human entities also known as hybrids are on the rise.

those from a strobe light—flickering from the bottom.

Then things got *really* strange.

So strange, in fact, that the next thing Dolan knew, he was back in his car, driving on the road and heading for home. The UFO was gone.

Dolan had trouble sleeping that night. For about a week, he woke up in the middle of each night, confused, sweating, and with his heart

> "The result of the hypnotic session indicated that Dolan had experienced an abduction during his sighting."

pounding. Somehow, some way, thought Dolan, that UFO had something to do with his sleeping problem.

Imbrogno interviewed Dolan and recommended hypnosis. Dr. Jean Mundy, a New York City psychologist, said, "The result of the hypnotic session indicated that Dolan had experienced an abduction during his sighting."

According to Dr. Mundy, Dolan revealed some incredible things while under hypnosis. He said that when the UFO passed over his car, he was somehow drawn out of the car window and into the UFO, where he was laid on a table in a dark rom. Several grayish-white creatures stood on each side of him, and one held some sort of tool and kept moving it around Dolan's head. Dolan tried to move but couldn't.

One of the aliens shoved something up his nose. "While remembering this part," said Imbrogno, "Dolan began to cry out in pain and his nose began to get red and swell."

> After checking out the control panel, the next thing he remembers is driving home.

Dolan, still under hypnosis, continued with his story, saying he was next allowed to get off the table and walk around. One creature showed him a control panel with a bunch of knobs and buttons. "At no time was there any talking, but Dolan knew where they wanted him to go and what they wanted him to do."

Dolan's story ends there. After checking out the control panel, the next thing he remembers is driving home.

Another person who claims to have been taken aboard a spacecraft in the Hudson Valley spoke of a similar experience. Bill Murphy, who was also interviewed by Imbrogno after suffering unusual nightmares following a UFO sighting in 1984, was eventually hypnotized and found to have had his own Close Encounter of the Fourth Kind. Here's what he had to say while he was hypnotized:

"I see it now. It's that thing! It's coming in my direction! I am going to turn off my car lights, and maybe then it won't see me and it'll go away. It's *huge*.

Oh my God, what is it? There's someone standing in the road. He is now walking toward the car. Who are you? He's saying something to me. 'Don't be fearful. We need you. You have been selected.' Selected for what? Get away. I feel strange, like I am floating in the

Extraterrestrial Contact Is Illegal

Meet E.T., go to jail. A little-known 1969 federal law outlaws any contact between a U.S. citizen and an extraterrestrial being. Break this law and you could spend a year in jail—and pay a $5,000 fine!

NO CONTACT

air. It's all dark. I am now on this table and these guys are all around me, six of them. Two are at my head, and two on each side of me. My legs and arms are like dead weights. I can't move them."

Bill then talks about what the space aliens were doing to him. "The one at my head is moving some type of device that looks like a portable car–vacuum–cleaner up and down the left side of my head. It vibrates my entire head. It feels like a drill going through my head. Stop! It hurts. He tells me that they are looking for something and found it."

The aliens then showed Bill a control panel and told him they'd see him again. "They told me that they need

us because they have trouble living in our world," Bill said under hypnosis. "They said they come from a place that is very ugly when compared to our world, and they would rather live here but can't."

Since his hypnosis, Bill remembers everything clearly. Before, he didn't recall a thing.

The first witness, Dolan, feels certain the aliens will come back someday. And his entire life has changed.

"He feels as if he is in some form of mental contact with the beings that he met," according to Imbrogno. "He feels as if he is gathering information for them. For example, he may be listening to music, and a voice inside his head will say, 'Tell us about this music. How does it make you feel?' He cannot control these questions. They can come at any time while he is experiencing something in his everyday life."

> The aliens then showed Bill a control panel and told him they'd see him again.

Pretty freaky, isn't it?

"This case is unusual, but not unique when compared to the many cases that I have investigated in the Hudson Valley," said Imbrogno. "The evidence indicates that there is some type of nonhuman intelligence at work. If the case histories are true, then we all better work together to get to the bottom of this."

CASE NO. 16:

Allagash

Here's a story that'll make you think twice before going on a canoe ride in the middle of the night.

In 1976, four men spent two weeks in August

camping along the Allagash Wilderness Waterway in northern Maine. On their second night out, twins Jim and Jack Weiner, along with friends Chuck Rak and Charlie Foltz, set up camp on Eagle Lake. It turned into a night they'll never forget.

After dark, Jim noticed a bright object in sky. "It was just floating over the treetops," he said. "It didn't seem to be moving in any direction. I looked at it through the binoculars for maybe fifteen or thirty seconds, and it just suddenly winked out from the outside edges inward. It was gone. I thought maybe it was a weather balloon or a helicopter that had its light off. But there was something about it that left me with an odd feeling."

Two nights later, on Thursday, August 26, they decided to go night fishing. Before paddling out in a canoe, the men built a huge bonfire at their campsite. The light would help them find their way back in the dark.

It turned into a night they'll never forget.

All four men rode in one canoe. No other campers were nearby. But were they alone?

On the lake, Chuck had a strange feeling that someone was staring at him from behind. "I turned over my right shoulder and I saw this large round globe of light that looked exactly like what we'd seen two nights previously," he said.

The men all turned to look. "It looked like a miniature sun, very, very bright," said Jim. "It lit the treetops up like it was daylight. And it was absolutely silent."

For some reason, Charlie picked up a flashlight and blinked it at the UFO. Uh-oh. It responded by whooshing right toward them. Frightened, the men splashed and thrashed their paddles in the water trying to race back to shore. "I never looked back," Charlie admitted.

As with most Close Encounters of the Fourth Kind,

the men didn't remember what happened after that. Their next memory was of being back on shore, staring up at the bright object, which was just a stone's throw away. "It seemed to shrink, then it reappeared up higher, even smaller, and then it just streaked away," said Jim. "In a few seconds it was like a star, just another star in the sky."

Chuck remembers stepping out of the canoe, going back to the campsite, and feeling no panic. "We seemed very relaxed," he said.

Everyone agreed they were out on the lake for twenty

minutes. But the huge bonfire—which should have lasted for hours—was already a bunch of coals!

Tired, the men went to bed. The next day they got up and moved on to their next campsite, as though nothing had happened. For the next ten days they fished and camped, but they saw no more of the UFO.

Years passed. The men told friends what had happened, but no one believed them. They could hardly believe it themselves.

Then the nightmares started. Jack had dreams in which he could see his brother and two friends sitting on a bench. "I was wondering why they weren't helping me, because I felt like I was in danger," he said. "And while I'm trying to figure this out, I noticed this dark, shadowy figure emerging from this bright light in front of me. I would wake up sweating, in a state of terror and shock."

> "In a few seconds it was like a star, just another star in the sky."

Jack told no one but his wife, Mary, about these dreams. But in 1988, he learned his brother Jim was having the same type of nightmares! Did they have anything to do with the bizarre light that had chased their canoe twelve years before?

Jim contacted UFO researcher Jim Fowler. Separately,

under hypnosis, all four men said they were taken aboard a craft where space aliens gave them a medical examination.

When the men learned that each had recalled the same experience in their hypnosis, they were stunned. "But it was kind of nice to know I wasn't going insane," said Jim. "The dreams were in fact real memories of an event that really happened."

Anthony Constantino, a professional hypnotist who worked with the four men, admits that hypnosis isn't always accurate. But he believes they were telling the truth. "After working with these guys, I was scared. I still am," he said. "I think they were being tagged—the way we tag and study sharks and bears and then release them. These are not four kooks. These are four decent, sincere human beings."

All four men also took lie detector tests. Although these tests aren't always accurate, either, they did indicate that all four men were telling the truth.

"This happened," insisted Charlie. "If you believe it, fine. If you don't believe it, I don't care. Because it did."

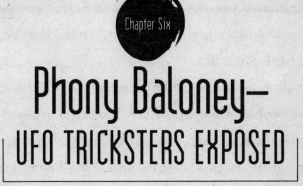

Chapter Six

Phony Baloney—
UFO TRICKSTERS EXPOSED

Way back in 1897, a man claimed he saw a spaceship land in Le Roy, Kansas. Strange beings stepped out, kidnapped a cow, and flew off, he said. As newspaper accounts spread word of the bizarre story, fearful citizens throughout the community went on alert.

ʀᴇᴀʟɪᴛʏ ᴄʜᴇᴄᴋ: The man eventually admitted he'd made up the whole story. Turns out he was a member of his town's liars' club, a group that competed to see who could tell the tallest tale.

Ask any ufologist and he'll tell you there's nothing more annoying than UFO hoaxes. Tricksters stage pranks with cleverly designed spaceship models or simply make up UFO stories to wreak havoc with serious investigation efforts. Even though they're rare (less than one out of every hundred UFO reports turns out to be faked), hoaxes present only dead ends that confuse the UFO issue and waste time. Unfortunately, they're a part of any ufologist's life.

Why do hoaxers do it? For starters, they think it's fun to fool people. (Beware of UFO reports around April Fools' Day!) And sure, it's easy enough to throw a hubcap in the air, snap a picture, and yell, "Flying saucer!" However, hoaxers usually crave attention more than anything, and through their tricks that's what they get. If they're really lucky, they can sell their phony stories to a book publisher or movie producer and make some big bucks.

Of course, hoaxers better hope they never really see a UFO. Remember the story about the boy who cried wolf? Once someone is caught lying about a UFO, no one ever believes him again—even if he has a true story to tell.

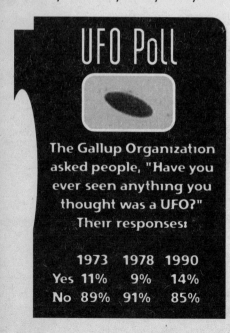

UFO Poll

The Gallup Organization asked people, "Have you ever seen anything you thought was a UFO?" Their responses:

	1973	1978	1990
Yes	11%	9%	14%
No	89%	91%	85%

While any number of unexplained UFOs could be the work of unknown hoaxers, here's a look at several cases that we're certain—or nearly certain—are fakes.

Roswell Autopsy Film

You already know about the most famous UFO case of them all, the Roswell crash. Even though it unfolded fifty years ago, the story has a life of its own, and new versions keep popping up, adding to and confusing the legend.

In 1995, a dramatic new piece of evidence emerged: a film that shows two doctors examining one of the dead aliens rumored to have been either captured or found dead at the famous flying saucer crash sight in 1947.

> The film shows two doctors examining one of the dead aliens.

The seventeen-minute black-and-white film aired on television across the world and sparked renewed interest in the old case. Viewers saw a naked humanoid creature with a bloated stomach lying on an operating table. In the film, the being has six fingers and a deep gash in its right leg. The alien's face looks lifeless, and its eerie eyes stare blankly at nothing. Two doctors, their faces hidden in special anticontamination suits, examine the creature with medical tools as a third person writes notes. Another human watches from behind a window, but you can't see this person's masked face.

UFO buffs jumped all over this film. Some claimed final proof of the Roswell cover-up had at long last arrived, while others said the film was a clever fake. Others

declared it real, but not from Roswell. One theory went so far as to say the film was faked by the government with hopes it would be declared a fake by ufologists. That way, goes the theory, no one would believe the truth—that a real autopsy actually took place.

> **Some claimed final proof of the Roswell cover-up had at long last arrived, while others said the film was a clever fake.**

An Englishman named Ray Santilli owns the film. He claimed he purchased it in 1992 from a former army photographer who was present at the autopsy,

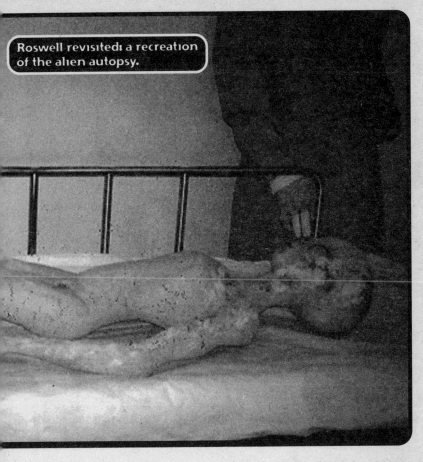

which supposedly took place at Fort Worth Army Air Field in Texas. "The whole thing was just way too fascinating to let go," said Santilli. The mystery cameraman has remained in the shadows, but Santilli thinks he may eventually step forward.

The film is an amazing attention-grabber. But is it real? The film has plenty of problems that would lead

Are You a Believer?

According to a 1990 Gallup Poll:
Almost half of all Americans believe intelligent life exists in outer space.
About one-third believe UFOs have landed on Earth.

you to question its authenticity. For example:

___ The film goes in and out of focus throughout the autopsy, and nearly every detailed close-up of the alien is blurred.

___ The film is interrupted several times by cuts. These seem to indicate that some footage has been removed or that the hoaxers did a sloppy job of editing.

___ A wall clock in the autopsy room indicates the procedure lasted two and one half hours. Medical experts say an autopsy of such major importance would have to take much longer.

___ No human faces can be seen in the footage.

___ The type of wall phone seen in the film was not manufactured before 1956.

___ No verification has been made that all of the footage was taken in 1947.

When the footage aired in the United States as *Alien Autopsy: Fact or Fiction?*, the show included interviews with film and special effects experts. Each of them judged the film and gave their opinions about whether it looked real or fake. Their conclusion? Uncertain. But some of those interviewed insist their comments were not quoted correctly. They believe the alien is either a dummy or a deformed human.

Kevin Randle, a UFO investigator who studied the case closely, believes space aliens landed or crashed near

> "The alien-autopsy film is a hoax."

Roswell. But the film? "The alien-autopsy film is a hoax," he insists. Steve Johnson, a Hollywood special effects designer who has created fake aliens for movies such as *Species* and *The Abyss*, agrees. He says it looks "pretty phony," but his statement was cut from the television show. Could Santilli and the producers have stacked the evidence in their favor?

Stan Winston, another movie effects designer who worked on *Jurassic Park* and *Aliens*, is seen on the show talking about how great the alien looks. But in magazine interviews later, Winston admits he told the show's producers he didn't believe it was real. "Do I think it's a hoax? Absolutely," he says. These remarks were not aired as part of the show.

"There's not a shred of evidence that it's a fake," responds Santilli. Maybe so, but there's not much evidence that it's real, either. Even the video, now available in stores, comes with a disclaimer. *We cannot currently warrant that the contents were filmed in 1947,* part of it reads. *Although our medical reports suggested that the creature is not human, this cannot be verified. Although we have been informed that the footage emanates from the Roswell incident, this has not yet been verified.*

Don't expect the controversy to die down any time soon. It's anybody's guess as to what the next chapter in the Roswell legend will be.

HOAX CASE № 2:

George Adamski

George Adamski took pictures of flying saucers with elaborate domes and windows back in the 1950s. He also claimed to be communicating with space aliens, and he even drove out into the California desert one day to meet one. He took friends, but they had to wait nearly a mile away while Adamski chatted with his visiting friend from Venus. Adamski returned with a story about meeting a humanoid-type being with long blond hair. They spoke in sign language and through mental telepathy, Adamski said.

A best-selling book came next. *Flying Saucers Have Landed* appeared in 1953 and was followed by several more books in which Adamski told outrageous stories of his visits to the moon. Adamski became so famous that he even headed to Europe and in 1963 met the Queen of Holland.

Two years later he died, and with him went his stories. Today, most ufologists agree that his pictures were crude, simple fakes and that his stories had to be lies. Scientists laugh at Adamski's descriptions of the moon and other planets, saying they were ridiculously impossible. And since Adamski pursued fame and fortune through his UFO stories, he has little credibility. It all adds up to one word: hoax!

HOAX CASE No. 3:

Billy Meier

As a young man, Billy Meier made some of the most outrageous UFO claims ever heard. He not only produced dozens of clear, color photographs of spaceships hovering near his farm in Switzerland, but he also claimed he'd had numerous meetings with space aliens. A female space alien he called Semjase told Meier she was from ERRA, a planet in the Pleiades star cluster.

Nearly every UFO book mentions the now-famous Meier, who has put together several books about his close encounters. (Uh-oh, major warning sign!) Prominent ufologist Dr. Jacques Vallee, among others, doesn't buy any of the stories. In 1989 Vallee visited Meier, who is now a wealthy media celebrity. He says analysis of Meier's photos indicates the presence of models suspended in the air by strings.

Plenty of folks love and believe Meier's UFO stories, even though Semjase and her alien friends no longer visit or communicate with him.

Most ufologists think Meier is the ultimate UFO hoaxer. "I've never met the man, but I say it's a hoax," says one. "He once had a hobby of building models, including spaceships. When I looked at one of his home movies of what was supposed to be a saucer passing a tree, it seemed impossible that it was a structured vehicle. The film was very bad, and it looked like a model. But his story lives on."

Doug and Dave

So far we've seen lots of UFO trickery: faked film, suspended models, made-up stories. But wait, there's more. Like phony crop circles. In 1991, two Englishmen—Doug Bower and David Chorley—made headlines by admitting they had created circles by sneaking around fields with cutting tools late at night. They'd gotten quite good at this and fooled many people, especially in their country, where more crop circles appear than anywhere else.

When the truth was revealed, some ufologists felt they had an explanation for *all* crop circles. Some even said Bower and Chorley had traveled the world making crop circles everywhere. But how could all crop circles be a hoax? At the very same time Doug and Dave were confessing on television in London, crop circles were forming in Canada, the United States, and at least fifteen other countries. It doesn't seem likely that these two men, or even a team of hoaxers, could possibly have created the thousands of crop circles still being found around the world.

The sneaky duo admitted as much. They confessed to

> **Even hoaxers who confess their crimes can end up making things worse.**

cutting only about two hundred circles, "just for the fun of it," they said. But this hoax demonstrates two troubling problems faced by ufologists. First, the hoaxers were not caught by anyone. Instead, they came forward on their own. Perhaps the truth would still be unknown if they hadn't. Second, once Doug and Dave confessed, too many people quickly—and incorrectly, it turns out—assumed they had an answer to all crop circles. Even hoaxers who confess their crimes can end up making things worse.

Chapter Seven

The Truth Is Out There—
UFO INVESTIGATORS

What can be done about all those unsolved UFO cases out there? Investigate!

Just about anyone can dive into the mystery. Ever since the first UFOs appeared, three types of investigators have searched for evidence and answers: the government and military, scientists, and members of various UFO investigative groups. We'll take a look at each.

Government and Military Investigations

The story of UFO investigations starts with the U.S. Air Force. Here's a quick debriefing to give you the background.

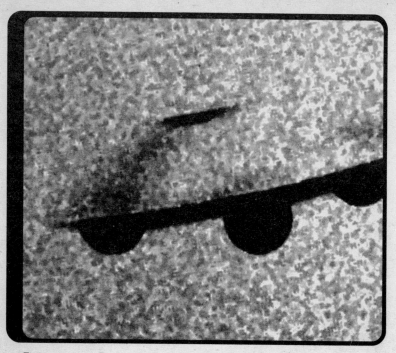

In 1947—the year of both the Roswell crash and Kenneth Arnold's "flying saucer" report—the Air Force started secretly analyzing UFO reports. Project Sign, which was later renamed Project Grudge, issued a 600-page report covering 244 UFO cases. The Air Force classified fifty-six of them as "unexplained."

With more than 1,500 UFOs reported in 1952, the Air Force had plenty to investigate, including dramatic sightings over the U.S. Capitol in Washington, D.C. An expanded Project Grudge became Project Blue Book, known today as one of the biggest UFO studies ever.

After reviewing nearly 25,000 sightings, the Blue Book investigation concluded that most cases were easily explained. The project shut down in 1969. UFOs posed no threat to national security, the Air Force stated, and there was no evidence that aliens were behind UFO reports.

> The Blue Book investigation concluded that most cases were easily explained.

Many people found this hard to believe, including Blue Book's chief scientist, Allen Hynek, who was also chairman of the department of astronomy at Northwestern University. Hynek could not explain every case as easily as the Air Force did. He claimed the Air Force just turned its head when a real UFO puzzle came along. "It would be bad public relations for the Air Force to admit there were things going on in the air over which they claim mastery," he said. In 1973, Hynek founded his own research group in Chicago, the Center for UFO Studies.

The Condon Committee

Other government studies came and went; none found evidence of aliens. Most of these projects were shrouded in secrecy.

In 1966, another major wave of sightings and encounters occurred. Senator (and later President) Gerald Ford, hoping to settle the mystery once and for all, started another UFO investigation with the Air Force. They appointed Dr. Edward Condon, a known UFO skeptic, to head the team. It came as no surprise that, two years later, his findings downplayed the phenomenon. The Condon Report examined only eighty-seven cases. And even though he couldn't explain 25 percent of the sightings, Condon told the government to quit the UFO investigation business. He said there just wasn't any mystery to study.

> In 1966, another major wave of sightings and encounters occurred.

Government Studies Today

The U.S. government and military no longer study UFOs. At least not officially.

"We do not actively investigate UFOs," Air Force Major Dave Thurston said. "We did so for twenty years and we found nothing. Since 1969, nothing has been brought to our attention to change our position."

UFO Organizations

CSICOP
(Committee for the Scientific Investigation of Claims of the Paranormal)

A group of skeptics who investigate unexplained mysteries and UFO encounters in an attempt to debunk and explain them scientifically.
Address: P.O. Box 703, Buffalo, NY 14226

CUFOS
(J. Allen Hynek Center for UFO Studies)

An international group of scientists and UFO investigators that receives and studies UFO reports. Also maintains a huge UFO library.
Address: 2457 W. Peterson Ave., Chicago, IL 60659

FUFOR
(Fund for UFO Research)

A nonprofit group of serious scientists who conduct research into the UFO phenomenon.
Address: P.O. Box 277, Mt. Rainier, MD 20712

MUFON
(Mutual UFO Network)

Largest UFO organization in the world. Members study and investigate cases, publish reports, and hold conferences about every possible UFO-related topic.
Address: 103 Oldtowne Road, Seguin, TX 78155

Thurston said he still gets calls from people who wish to report a UFO sighting. Standard procedure requires him to refer these callers to either the Federal Aviation Administration or to the local police. No such call, according to Thurston, has involved national security, and that's why the Air Force doesn't take the reports.

Some ufologists think the CIA now secretly handles the Air Force's old task of UFO research. The CIA insists that it doesn't.

The National Aeronautics and Space Administration (NASA) briefly got involved with space alien studies from 1992-93. The project, called Search for Extraterrestrial Intelligence, or SETI, planned to use high-tech radio telescopes to scan the skies. Scientists hoped to pick up any unusual electronic signals that might be coming from intelligent life elsewhere in the universe. Congress stopped funding the project in 1993, but NASA still receives ten to twelve calls each week about UFOs. "It's the most-asked question we get," says a space agency spokesman.

The Scientists

Most scientists scoff at the notion of UFOs. "Where's the proof?" they snicker. But plenty of them believe in the *possibility* of extraterrestrial life. And there are quite a few scientific projects now searching the far reaches of the universe for a sign of it.

Instead of looking, however, they listen. Gigantic radio telescopes that look like TV satellite

> A radio telescope on Earth, if pointed in the right direction, might pick up the noise.

dishes (except they're up to one thousand feet in diameter) are pointed at the sky. Astronomers tune in and listen. They're hoping to find fluctuations in the radio

UFO Hot Spots in the U.S.

GULF BREEZE, FLORIDA:
Resident Ed Walters's 1988
UFO photographs started a
flap that continues today.

**HUDSON VALLEY,
NEW YORK:**
More than 7,000 UFO
reports have come out of
this area in the past eight years.

ELMWOOD, WISCONSIN:
One of the many rural U.S. towns that calls itself
"UFO Capital of the World."

RACHEL, NEVADA:
Area 51's next-door neighbor.

ROSWELL, NEW MEXICO:
The famous crash took place more than fifty years
ago, but the faithful still flock to this town's two
UFO museums.

SEDONA, ARIZONA:
Believed to be one of only twenty-two "vortex
centers" in the world, this place attracts New Age
types who believe the red rocks and natural
magnetic fields make it a UFO haven.

YAKIMA, WASHINGTON:
Strange lights abound. So do bigfoot sightings.

waves from distant sources that might indicate intelligent alien life. If an alien race on another planet has similar radio technology, it might be beaming signals into space. A radio telescope on Earth, if pointed in the right direction, might pick up the noise.

> So far, they've heard nothing unusual.

Radio telescope efforts with names like Project Phoenix, Big Ear, and the SETI League are listening in on a lot of galaxies from around the universe. So far, they've heard nothing unusual.

"But we don't do any sort of UFO research," says an astronomer with Project Phoenix. "There's just no physical evidence whatsoever. No one ever comes in my office with a knob from a UFO. I wish they would, because it would make my job a lot easier."

The Fund

One group of scientists thinks differently. Since 1979 the Fund for UFO Research, also known as "The Fund," has raised money for scientists working on serious UFO research projects. "We don't care what the truth is," says Don Berliner, a member of the Fund's Executive Committee, "but the only way to find it is to be scientific." So far, the Fund has spent nearly $500,000 to support a half-dozen projects, including a study of abduction victims and the Roswell case.

According to Berliner, the most compelling evidence that space aliens are behind UFOs would be radar/visual (R-V) cases. These are cases in which somebody actually sees a UFO (the visual part) at the same time the UFO appears in the same place on a radar screen (the radar part). The radar observation confirms the witness's report. Usually, you only get one or the other, but there are about one hundred R-V cases on record. One sighting occurred recently in northern New Mexico. A jet pilot noticed three 400-foot cigar-shaped objects below his plane. They were confirmed by mili-

"We don't care what the truth is."

tary radar—but not explained, according to Berliner.

The R-V cases on record indicate UFOs that perform in highly unusual ways, like silent hovering followed by extreme acceleration. Some indicate odd-shaped craft unlike any airplane ever seen. Radar has tracked cylindrical objects flying level at low speed and round objects flying at high speed.

Couldn't these be secret military planes?

Advanced radar tracks everything in the sky.

"I don't think so," Berliner says. "If they were, we wouldn't be building airplanes as we know them today. And can you imagine the difficulty of keeping all this secret? That would be an extremely exciting secret. You'd have to tell someone or explode! It's hard to imagine no leaks."

Berliner doesn't buy the military explanation for another reason: the witnesses he has interviewed. "I've talked to enough military pilots who've chased these things, and their awe is so great, and frightening," he says. "They don't speak out publicly. But they're as curious as anyone, especially when they're flying the hottest thing the Air Force has, and they encounter something way off the scale."

Sounds like an exciting mystery that should interest any scientist. So why aren't more of them interested? "There are a lot more scientists involved than you may think," says Berliner. "But they just keep quiet, out of fear of the public making fun of them."

Other UFO Groups

Just about anyone can investigate UFOs. Unfortunately, that can be a problem. Many freelancers are poorly trained, or worse yet, they're flying saucer fans. They *want* every sighting to be an alien craft.

> The only good investigator is one who is willing to look at every possible answer and accept only those proven beyond a shadow of a doubt.

The only good investigator is one who is willing to look at every possible answer and accept only those proven beyond a shadow of a doubt. Yet many private investigators assume space aliens are the *only* answer to strange sightings. They waste a lot of time yelling about government cover-ups and conspiracies and focusing on bizarre stories like Billy Meier's.

On the World Wide Web, you can find hundreds of

Common Mistakes

You might say "Duh" when you find out what
some UFOs turn out to be. Yet these things fool
people, and someday they could fool you, too.

HEAVENLY BODIES
•The moon, planets, and stars. Don't laugh.
Sometimes planets and stars seem to wiggle and
shine green, blue, or red. That's because a star's
light bends as it travels through the Earth's
atmosphere, accounting for the unusual effect.

BIZARRE WEATHER
•Clouds. Some look exactly like a flying saucer.
Lenticular clouds—fat in the middle and thin on
the edges—fool people all the time. Others, called
noctilucent clouds, reflect light and appear to
be a lit spacecraft floating or hovering.

•Sun dogs and moon dogs (light that reflects off of
ice particles high up in the Earth's atmosphere)

•St. Elmo's fire   • Northern lights
•Ball lightning   •Swamp gas

AIRCRAFT
•Weather balloons
•Satellites   •Military aircraft   •Helicopters
•Birds

UFO groups, theorists, and so-called investigators spreading ridiculous rumors. Unfortunately, many people take them seriously.

Then there are anti-UFO groups. They devote their efforts to proving that every UFO sighting is a mistake or hoax. One such group, the Committee for the Scientific Investigation of Claims of the Paranormal (CSICOP), insists that space aliens and UFOs do not exist. CSICOP investigators do a terrific job of explaining everything from ghosts to UFOs, but, just like someone who desperately wants to believe in UFOs, they've already made up their minds before they investigate.

That's not good enough.

"You have to follow the facts to *wherever* they lead," says Linda Moulton-Howe.

Several large UFO organizations consist of people across the country who, like Moulton-Howe, investigate close encounters on their own. They're better trained and organized than most freelancers who go it alone, and they work together to gather information and file reports in a consistent way. In other words, they're more scientific.

The oldest and largest group is the Mutual UFO Network, or MUFON. It is one of the three top UFO groups in the nation (along with Hynek's Center for

UFO Studies and The Fund). The 5,000-member network investigates sightings around the world and files reports with MUFON headquarters in Seguin, Texas, where an amazing amount of information is stored and analyzed. Members, who pay $25 to join, also attend meetings and conventions to review the latest UFO research and receive the monthly *MUFON UFO Journal*. The group has also put together an impressive *Field Investigator's Manual*, which covers just about everything a UFO investigator needs to know. MUFON investigators are tested and trained with this guidebook.

How You Can Investigate UFOs

Two prominent ufologists, Walt Webb and Dan Wright, have investigated UFO sightings for decades. Like many investigators, both became involved with UFO research after they'd had their own close encounters. Wright also helped write the *MUFON Field Investigator's Manual*. In general, they advise all investigators to note the following:

🐾 Always approach a case as though it's logically explainable. Never make up your mind in advance! Webb, for example, has a list of about eighty IFOs and phenomena that are misinterpreted as alien craft. It's the first thing he consults on a case.

● A background in astronomy, engineering, or science always comes in handy.

● Beware of hoaxes. With experience, you'll pick up on the warning signs. Ask other people about the witness. If they all say, "Oh, that guy tells stories," then he's probably telling another one. Closely examine evidence, especially photographs, for signs of fakery.

● Treat witnesses with respect. They're often afraid and unsure of what they saw. Be considerate of their feelings and their requests for privacy.

Happy Hunting

Now that you know what it takes to investigate the greatest mystery of our time, get busy. Happy hunting, and keep your eyes on the skies—you never know what you might see. . . .

UFO FILES

Investigator's Field Kit

T hink you're up for your own UFO investigation? First, calm down! Then follow these steps:

1. Interview all witnesses separately. Conduct interviews away from the sighting location, and ask for permission to tape-record. First, let each witness tell his or her story. Ask questions only after they're finished. Be open to what you hear.

2. Have witnesses write down their statements and sign them. Give them a copy.

3. Visit the scene of the encounter and mark it on a map. Have the witnesses retrace the sighting by pointing out where the object was seen, what it did, and how long it was visible. Use an ele-

What to Take UFO Hunting

❑ Tape measure for evidence like pod marks and landing spots

❑ Tape recorder and batteries

❑ Camera with flash and tripod

❑ A six-inch and a twelve-inch rule, and coins of four different sizes. (Witness can use a coin, held at arm's length, to determine the relative size of a UFO)

❑ Sighting compass to sight on a landmark

❑ Inclinometer to measure altitude

❑ Map of area that shows all streets, landmarks, and topography

❑ Notebook, pen, and drawing pad for witness sketches

❑ Official forms to fill out

❑ An open mind!

vation and sighting compass to fix the object's altitude and position in the sky.

4. Look for physical evidence. It's extremely rare, but you should look.

5. Pay close attention to witnesses' behavior. Are they genuinely afraid? Do they have prior UFO experiences? What do they *think* they saw?

6. Look for other witnesses in the neighborhood who might have seen the object. The more you have, the better. Check witnesses' credibility with people who know them.

7. Check weather, astronomical data, airport schedules, balloon launchings, and other possible explanations in the area.

8. Write up a detailed report of the case and your investigation. Attach witness statements, photos, and any relevant info. File it or turn it over to a credible investigative group. As you compile more reports, compare them. Over time, you'll detect trends and other valuable tidbits that will help you conduct future investigations.

Out of This World Contest

Are there really such things as aliens, UFOs, ghosts, or the undead?

Have you—or someone you know—ever seen any visitors from out of this world?

Tell us all about a true close encounter—or a ghost encounter—and you could get your terrifying tale published in *Disney Adventures* magazine!

ENTRY FORM

Name _____

Address _____

City _____ State ____ Zip_____

Area Code _____ Phone Number _____

Birth Date: Month _____ Day ____ Year _____

I did not have any help completing this *Out of This World* story.

Your signature

_____

One of your parents' or guardians' signatures on the line below.

_____

Write your Out of This World story about a true encounter with a ghost or a UFO in 250 words or less and send it to:

Disney Adventures/
Out of This World Contest
P.O. Box 864
New York, NY 10113-0864

Send your entry by December 31, 1997. You must be at least 7 years old but not more than 14 years old by December 31, 1997, to enter.

OUT OF THIS WORLD CONTEST RULES

NO PURCHASE NECESSARY

1. HOW TO ENTER: Staple the completed entry form, or a 3" x 5" card with your full name, address (city, state, or province and zip or mail code), daytime phone number (with area code), and your date of birth, to the upper left corner of the first page of your story and mail it, postage prepaid, to DISNEY ADVENTURES/Out of This World Contest, P. O. Box 864, New York, NY 10113-0864. All entries must be postmarked by December 31, 1997. (Mechanically reproduced entry forms are acceptable.) The story must be true and should be no longer than 250 words. Winners will be chosen on the basis of creativity and originality.

2. ENTRY LIMITATIONS: Only one entry per person. Open only to children between the ages of 7 and 14, as of December 31, 1997, who are legal residents of the U.S. (excluding its territories, possessions, overseas military installations, and commonwealth) or Canada (excluding Quebec), and are not employees of Disney Magazine Publishing, Inc. (the "Sponsor"), its parent or affiliated companies, the advertising, promotional, or fulfillment agencies of any of them, nor members of their immediate families. Sponsor is not responsible for printing errors or inaccurate, incomplete, stolen, lost, illegible, mutilated, postage-due, misdirected, delayed, or late entries or mail.

3. RESERVATIONS: Void where prohibited or restricted by law and subject to all federal, state, provincial, and local laws and regulations. All entries become the Sponsor's property and will not be returned, and may be reprinted without further consent or compensation. By entering this contest, each entrant agrees to be bound by these rules and the decisions of the judges. Acceptance of prize constitutes the grant of an unconditional right to use winner's name and/or likeness for any and all publicity, advertising, and promotional purposes without additional compensation, except where prohibited by law. Sponsor is not responsible for claims, injuries, losses, or damages of any kind resulting from the acceptance, use, misuse, possession, loss, or misdirection of any prize.

4. WINNERS: Winners will be notified by mail on or about January 31, 1998. The failure of a potential winner's parents/legal guardian to verify address and execute and return an Affidavit of Eligibility/Release within 10 days from the date of notification, or the return of a notification as undeliverable, will result in disqualification and the selection of an alternate winner. For the name of the winner (after January 31, 1998) and/or contest rules, send a self-addressed, stamped envelope to DISNEY ADVENTURES/Out of This World Contest Winner, 114 Fifth Avenue, New York, NY 10011-5690. WA and VT residents may omit the return postage.

5. PROCEDURES: Contest begins on October 7, 1997, and ends on December 31, 1997. Odds of winning depend on the number of eligible entries received and the quality of the entries.

6. PRIZE: One (1) Grand Prize: Winner receives publication of his/her story in the June issue of *Disney Adventures*. The prize will be awarded.